A NOTE TO PARENTS

When your children are ready to "step into reading," giving them the right books is as crucial as giving them the right food to eat. **Step into Reading Books** and STAR WARS® **JEDI READERS** present exciting stories and information reinforced with lively, colorful illustrations that make learning to read fun, satisfying, and worthwhile. They are priced so that acquiring an entire library of them is affordable. And they are beginning readers with a difference—they're written on five levels.

Early Step into Reading Books are designed for brand-new readers, with large type and only one or two lines of very simple text per page. **Step 1 Books** feature the same easy-to-read type as the Early Step into Reading Books, but with more words per page. **Step 2 Books** are both longer and slightly more difficult, while **Step 3 Books** introduce readers to paragraphs and fully developed plot lines. **Step 4 Books** offer exciting fiction and nonfiction for the increasingly independent reader.

The grade levels assigned to the five steps—preschool through kindergarten for the Early Books, preschool through grade 1 for Step 1, grades 1 through 3 for Step 2, grades 2 through 3 for Step 3, and grades 2 through 4 for Step 4—are intended only as guides. Some children move through all five steps very rapidly; others climb the steps over a period of several years. Either way, these books will help your child "step into reading" in style!

www.randomhouse.com/kids
www.starwars.com

Library of Congress Cataloging-in-Publication Data
Krulik, Nancy E.
Jar Jar's mistake / by Nancy Krulik ; illustrated by Richard Walz.
p.   cm. — (Jedi readers. A step 1 book)
SUMMARY: Accident-prone Jar Jar Binks has adventures and mishaps
in the Mos Espa marketplace on the planet Tatooine.
ISBN 0-375-80000-X (trade). — ISBN 0-375-90000-4 (lib. bdg.)
[1. Science fiction.] I. Walz, Richard, ill.   II. Title.   III. Series: Jedi Readers.
Step 1 book. PZ7.K944Jar 1999 [E]—dc21   98-48537

Printed in the United States of America 10 9 8 7 6 5 4 3 2 1
STEP INTO READING is a registered trademark of Random House, Inc.

STAR WARS

EPISODE I

JAR JAR'S MISTAKE

A Step 1 Book

by Nancy Krulik
illustrated by Richard Walz

Random House
New York

LUCAS BOOKS

This is Jar Jar Binks.
Jar Jar is hungry.
He goes to the market
to find food.

The market is big.

The market is busy.

Jar Jar is scared.

But he is *hungry*.

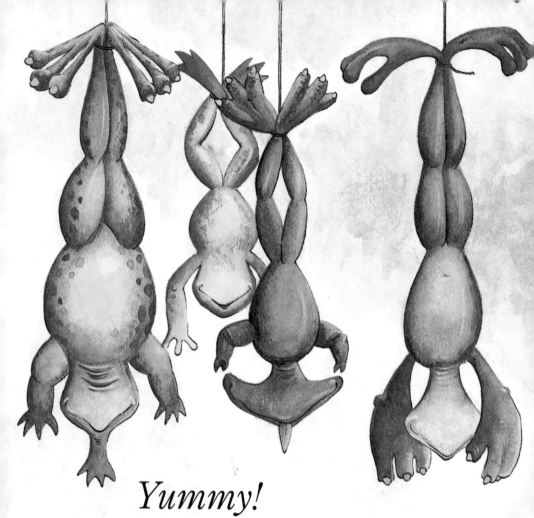

Yummy!

Jar Jar sees some
fat frogs for sale.
Gungans love
to eat frogs!

Slurp!

Jar Jar slurps up

a fat frog.

"Hey!"

yells the frog seller.

"You have to pay

for that!"

Jar Jar is surprised.

He opens his mouth.

Pop!

Out pops the frog.

It bounces all over.

Clunk!

The frog clunks

a Wookiee.

14

Clank!

It clanks
a droid
on the back.

Splash!

The frog
splashes into
a bowl of soup.

It is Sebulba's soup.

Sebulba is big.

Sebulba is mean.

And Sebulba is
very mad.

"Is this your frog?"

Sebulba asks Jar Jar.

Jar Jar is
very, very quiet.

Sebulba pushes
Jar Jar down.

Jar Jar closes his
eyes.
He does not
want to see
Sebulba's big fists.
"Stop!" someone says.

It is
Anakin Skywalker!
"Do not hurt Jar Jar,"
says Anakin.
"Jar Jar is a friend
of the Hutts."
The Hutts are bigger
and meaner
than Sebulba.

Now Sebulba is afraid!
Sebulba drops
his fists and
sneaks away.

Anakin helps
Jar Jar up.
Anakin is a
good friend.

"Be less afraid,"
Anakin says
to Jar Jar.
"Bullies pick on those
who are afraid."

Jar Jar smiles.

Now he feels brave.

But he is still hungry!